KAYA
1764

THE JOURNEY BEGINS

by Janet Shaw

☆ American Girl®

A Peek into
KAYA'S
WORLD

Kaya's tribe, the Nez Perce, traveled with the seasons. For most of the year, they built tepees covered with mats made from tule (TOO-lee) reeds. Each tepee housed one entire family—mother, father, children, grandparents, and visiting relatives. When it was time to move on, they simply took down the poles, rolled up the mats, and carried them to the next campsite.

KAYA'S FAMILY and FRIENDS

Toe-ta
Kaya's father, an expert horseman
and wise village leader

Eetsa
Kaya's mother, who is a good
provider for her family
and her village

Wing Feather
and Sparrow
Kaya's mischievous
twin brothers

Brown Deer
Kaya's older sister, who will soon
be old enough to marry

Speaking Rain
A blind girl who lives with
Kaya's family and is a sister to Kaya

Kalutsa and Aalah

Toe-ta's parents, who teach
Kaya the old ways

Pi-lah-ka and Kautsa

Eetsa's parents, who guide
and comfort Kaya

Steps High

Kaya's beloved horse

Two Hawks

A Salish boy who is a
friend to Kaya

Raven

A boy who loves to race horses

Fox Tail

A bothersome boy
who can be rude

KAYA

of the Nimíipuu People

Kaya and her family are Nimíipuu, known today as Nez Perce Indians. They speak the Nez Perce language, so you'll see some Nez Perce words in this book. "Kaya" is short for the Nez Perce name Kaya'aton'my,' which means "she who arranges rocks." You'll find the meanings and pronunciations of these and other Nez Perce words in the glossary on page 92.

TABLE of CONTENTS

LET'S RACE!

✸ Chapter 1 ✸

WHEN KAYA AND HER FAMILY RODE
over the hill in to *Wallowa*, The Valley of the Winding
Waters, her horse pricked up her ears and whinnied.
Answering whinnies came from the large herd grazing
nearby. Kaya stroked the smooth shoulder of her horse.

"Go easy, Steps High," she said softly. "We'll be there soon."

It was midsummer, the season when salmon swam
upstream to the lake to lay their eggs. Many bands of
Nimíipuu gathered here each year to catch and dry the

salmon. Kaya and her family were traveling with several other families from Salmon River Country to join the fishing. Kaya loved these reunions with her grandparents and her many other relatives, old and young—all the children were like brothers and sisters to one another.

Steps High whinnied again and began to prance, stepping high just like her name. Kaya held tight to the lead rope of the old pony that her sister Speaking Rain rode. A sickness in Speaking Rain's eyes had caused her to lose her sight.

"Your horse wants to run!" Speaking Rain said to Kaya.

As if the horse understood Speaking Rain's words, Steps High tossed her head and pawed the ground. Kaya rubbed Steps High's sleek neck. "If only we could race, I know we'd beat all the others!"

Eetsa, Kaya's mother, turned to look Kaya in the eye. "I've told you before not to boast," she said firmly. "Our actions speak for us. Our deeds show our worth. Let that be your lesson, Kaya."

Kaya pressed her lips together—she knew Eetsa was right.

❊◈❊

When Kaya and her family rode up, her grandmother, *Aalah*, was waiting at the doorway of her family's tepee. Aalah stepped forward. Her face was creased with age, and little pockmarks, like fingerprints, covered her cheeks.

"*Tawts may-we!*" she said. "Welcome, all of you!"
Smiling, she hugged Kaya and Speaking Rain as soon
as they climbed off their horses. Kaya's twin brothers,
Sparrow and Wing Feather, giggled as they scampered to
hide behind a travois and peeked at Aalah, their dark eyes
gleaming.

"Look how these boys
have grown," Aalah said as
the twins ran from their hiding
spot into her outstretched arms.
"So full of laughter and tricks!
Keep a sharp eye on these little
ones, Kaya."

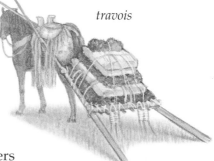

travois

Kaya nodded. Her little brothers
were harder to herd than wild ponies! They
ran everywhere and were curious about everything.

Kaya turned and saw her father, *Toe-ta*, gazing at the
herd of sleek horses, some of them spotted, in the wide
meadow. Perhaps Toe-ta was thinking of trading for some
of the horses, or of the races they'd have. He was an expert
horseman. Often he won races on his fleet-footed stallion,
Runner.

Kaya was certainly thinking about horse races. For a
long time she'd imagined being in one on her adored Steps
High. She knew Steps High was fast, but also young and

untested. Toe-ta had told her that Steps High wasn't ready to race yet.

Kaya and her older sister Brown Deer carried their bundles into the tepee and placed them across from where their grandparents slept. Speaking Rain stacked the bundles neatly along the wall of the tepee. It was always packed full when they gathered here. But Kaya liked it crowded and cozy, and the tule mats that covered the tepee let in cool breezes and light.

After the women and girls had put everything in order around the tepee, Eetsa allowed Kaya to take Speaking Rain and the little boys to play. "Remember, it's your job to look after your brothers carefully," she reminded Kaya.

Kaya knew there were dangerous animals about. She also knew about the Stick People—small mischievous people who might lure a child to wander too far away into the woods. *"Aa-heh,"* Kaya said. "I will."

She led Speaking Rain and the twins to a group of boys and girls gathered in the shade beside the river. Raven, a boy a little older than Kaya, was playing a game with a length of hemp cord.

"Here's what happened when Coyote went to put up his tepee," Raven said. The twins watched, wide-eyed, as Raven's fingers flashed, weaving the cord into the shape of a tepee. Then, with a tug, he made the tepee collapse.

"Coyote worked too fast!" he said. "He didn't tie the poles properly, and his tepee fell down on him!" Everyone laughed and the twins squealed at the fun.

Raven leaned back on his elbows in the thick grass. "I see you have a new horse, Little Sister," he said to Kaya. "She's a pretty one."

"She's the prettiest horse in the whole herd!" Kaya said. She couldn't disguise her pride. Steps High wasn't large, only about thirteen hands high. She had a black head and chest, a white rump with black spots on it, and a white star on her forehead. "She's fast, too," Kaya added. *That wasn't boasting,* she thought—just saying what was true.

Fox Tail squatted beside her. He was a bothersome boy who could be rude. He always followed Raven, trying to impress the older boy. "Your horse looks skittish to me," he said to Kaya. "Why would your father give you a horse like that?"

"Toe-ta didn't choose my horse," Kaya said. "My horse chose me."

Fox Tail laughed and slapped his leg. "Your horse chose you? How?"

"One day I was riding by the herd with Toe-ta," Kaya

※ 5 ※

said. "A filly kept nickering to me. So I whistled to her. She followed me. She came up to me and rubbed her head against my leg. Toe-ta said that meant she wanted to be my horse. He worked with me so I could ride her."

"Is that a true story?" Fox Tail demanded.

"Ask my father if that's true," Kaya said.

"I believe you," Raven said. "But you say she's fast. Should I believe that, too?"

"I haven't raced her yet, but I've run her many times," Kaya said. "She glides over the ground like the shadow of an eagle."

Fox Tail jumped to his feet. "Like an eagle—big talk!" he said. "Let's race our horses and see if yours flies like you claim she does!"

Kaya had an uneasy feeling. *I shouldn't have boasted about her speed,* she thought. *I've never raced her.* "My horse is tired now," she said hesitantly.

"She's not too tired for one short race," Fox Tail insisted. "Maybe your horse isn't so fast, after all."

Kaya felt her face grow hot. Her horse was as swift as the wind! She was sired by Toe-ta's fine stallion, Runner.

Kaya stood up. "Speaking Rain, could you take care of the twins for me?" she asked. "I know it's my job, but I want to race."

Speaking Rain was braiding strands of grass into

bracelets for the little boys. "I'll try, but sometimes they play tricks on me."

"I'll only be gone a little while," Kaya assured her.

THE STICK PEOPLE

※ Chapter 2 ※

Kaya, Raven, and Fox Tail got on their horses and rode up to the raised plain at the end of the lake. Often people held celebrations and races here on the level ground, but today Kaya and the boys were alone.

Now that she'd decided to race, Kaya was eager to begin. Steps High seemed eager, too. When Fox Tail's roan horse came close, Steps High arched her neck and flattened her ears. When Raven's chestnut horse passed her, she trotted faster.

Raven reined in his horse. "We'll start here. When I give the signal, we'll race until we pass that boulder at the far end of the field." He held his hand high. Then he brought it down and they were off!

The boys took the lead, stones spurting from under their horses' hooves. They lay low on their horses, with their weight forward. They ran neck and neck.

Steps High bolted after them but swung out too wide. Kaya pressed her heels into Steps High's sides. Then she gave Steps High her head, and her horse sprang forward.

Kaya thrilled to feel her horse gather herself, lengthen out, and gallop flat out. She was running as she'd never run before. Her long strides were so smooth that she seemed to be floating, her hooves barely touching the earth. Her dark mane whipped Kaya's face. Grit stung Kaya's lips. She clung to her horse, barely aware that they'd caught the other horses until they passed them. She and Steps High were in the lead!

Suddenly, Steps High began to buck! She plunged, head down, heels high. Kaya grasped the horse's mane and hung on. She bit her tongue and tasted blood. Steps High bucked again!

Raven quickly spun his horse around. He was beside Steps High in an instant and grabbed the reins. He pulled the horse sharply to him, and in the same motion, he halted his own horse. Steps High skidded to a standstill, foam lathering her neck. Kaya slid off.

Steps High's eyes were wild. For a moment she seemed never to have been tamed at all. Kaya's legs were shaking badly, but her first thought was to calm her horse. She began to stroke Steps High's trembling head and neck.

Fox Tail came galloping back. "I knew that horse was skittish!" he cried. "She just proved it."

"She proved she's fast, too," Raven said.

Kaya wanted to thank Raven for coming to her aid,

but her wounded pride was a knife in her chest. She could hardly get her breath. Leading her horse slowly to cool her down, Kaya silently walked away from the boys.

When Kaya had rubbed down Steps High, she turned her horse out to graze. Then she started back through the woods, heading toward the river.

Her feelings were all tangled up like a nest of snakes. She was excited that Steps High had run so fast, but she was disappointed that her horse had broken her training. Kaya was relieved that she hadn't been bucked off, but she wished the boys hadn't seen her lose control. She knew she shouldn't have boasted, but she also wished she could have made good on her boast and won the race.

When Kaya glanced up from nursing her hurt feelings, Fox Tail was coming down the trail toward her on foot. He stopped right in front of her. "You told us your horse chose you," he said with a smirk. "Would you choose her after the way she tried to buck you off today?"

"She's the best horse ever!" Kaya said. "She can run faster than your horse, and I can run faster than you, too. Want to race me right now?"

Fox Tail cocked his head. "The first one to the

riverbank wins!" he cried. He turned and sprinted away down the path.

For a little while Kaya was right on his heels. Then Fox Tail left the path, leaped over a fallen log, and took off through the woods. *He must know a shortcut,* Kaya thought. She followed him.

But she couldn't keep him in sight because he jagged in and out of shadows. Was that his dark head beyond the bushes? Now she was uncertain which way to go. She stopped to listen for the sound of the river as her guide.

She stood in a gloomy clearing surrounded by black willows. She listened for rushing water. There was only silence. No wind blew in the leaves, no flies buzzed. All Kaya could hear was her heartbeat.

Then a twig snapped behind her. She whirled around. Did something just duck behind that tree? The shadows around her seemed to waver and sway. Was it the Stick People? Had they led her to this part of the woods?

Kaya held her breath. She knew the Stick People were cunning and crafty. They were strong, too. She'd heard they could carry off a baby and leave it a long way from its mother.

A flock of jays cawed—or was it the Stick People signaling to her? They seemed to be saying, "Forgot! Forgot!" Kaya shivered. What had she forgotten?

Then she gasped. She'd forgotten her little brothers! Kaya should never have given her job to Speaking Rain. The little boys were four winters old, just the right age for mischief. Kaya must get back to them at once, before they got into danger.

She knew she must leave a gift for the Stick People in return for their help. They became angry with people who didn't treat them respectfully. She found rose hips in the bag she wore on her belt and placed them on the moss. Then she began running back the way she'd come.

SWITCHED!

Chapter 3

KAYA RAN ALONG THE RIVERBANK,

past women cleaning salmon and cutting the fish into thin strips. Auntie was laying the strips on racks to dry. She raised her hand in greeting when Kaya rushed by.

But Kaya kept going. She ran up to some girls setting up a little camp for their buckskin dolls. They'd made a travois with sticks and pieces of an old tule mat. A boy pretended to be their horse, pulling the travois. "Have you seen Speaking Rain and my brothers?" Kaya asked.

The children shook their heads, and Kaya ran on, desperate to find them.

The twins had never been like other little boys. They could understand each other without saying a word out loud. When they were born, the setting sun and the rising moon were both in the sky. Two lights in the sky and two babies who looked alike—they were special children. They could also be twice the trouble if they decided to play tricks.

Kaya ran through some brush and out onto the grassy bank where she'd last seen Speaking Rain with the boys.

Speaking Rain crouched by a twisted pine tree, but the twins were nowhere in sight.

"Where are the boys?" Kaya called.

"I don't know," Speaking Rain said. "But I just found the toy I made for them." She held up a little hoop made of grass. "They got tired of my game and ran off. I've been calling them but they don't answer." Her cloudy eyes were wide with alarm. "Maybe they fell in the river!"

Kaya caught her breath. "Did you hear a splash?"

Speaking Rain shook her head. "But where could they be? Maybe a cougar chased them."

Cougars! Cougars sometimes went after small children. Kaya's heart raced, but she tried not to let Speaking Rain feel her alarm. "Come on, let's look for the boys. If they just ran off, they can't be far." She made herself sound confident, but she was frightened. The boys could be hurt or lost. Oh, why hadn't she thought of them instead of herself?

Kaya looked around. Two trails led away from the river. One turned upstream toward where the women worked. The other turned downstream. Dust-covered leaves hung low over that trail. The boys would have been drawn to that leafy tunnel. "Boys!" Kaya called. "Where are you?"

There was no answer.

"Follow me," Kaya said to Speaking Rain. "I'll look, and you listen."

Speaking Rain took hold of Kaya's sleeve and walked right behind her down the trail.

"I see their footprints in the dust," Kaya said. She walked faster. "And here's where they left the trail and went under the bushes. They were crawling. We'll have to crawl, too. Stay close."

The girls got down on their hands and knees and inched forward. Leaves caught in their braids and brushed their cheeks. Kaya kept a lookout for the Stick People hiding in the shadows. Maybe they'd led the boys deeper into the woods.

A little farther on, the prints disappeared. Kaya sat back on her heels. "I've lost their trail. Do you hear anything?"

Speaking Rain lifted her chin and frowned. "I hear the river. There's swift water there. If the boys fell in, they'd be swept away."

Kaya put her hand on Speaking Rain's shoulder. "Let's keep looking," she said. She began to search for footprints again.

"I think we should get others to help us," Speaking Rain said. Then she pointed up. "Listen, I hear something up there!"

Kaya rose to her feet so that she could see over the bushes. An old spruce tree loomed overhead. A cougar might be crouching in the branches! Or the boys. She'd been so busy following signs on the ground that she'd forgotten the twins could climb trees.

A spruce branch trembled. Two pairs of dark eyes gazed down at her from the green boughs. The boys were clinging to the trunk like raccoons. They were grinning.

Kaya was flooded with relief. She was also angry that the boys had scared her and Speaking Rain. "Come down right now!" she said.

The little boys crept down out of the tree in a shower of dry needles. When they reached the ground, they started to giggle.

Kaya took their hands and crouched to look into their eyes. "Don't laugh!" she said. "Running off isn't a game. Dangers are everywhere!"

"Yes, dangers are everywhere," a low voice said.

Startled, Kaya and Speaking Rain turned. Someone was coming through the woods behind them.

Hands parted the branches, and Auntie stepped through. Her face was stern. "When you ran by me, I sensed trouble, so I followed you," she said. "Now I see I was right. I heard your mother tell you to look after your brothers. But you ran away from your responsibility."

Kaya felt her face redden. She bit her lips. Auntie's words made her ache with shame. "I'm sorry," she whispered.

"You should be sorry," Auntie said in a weary voice.

"I must call Whipwoman to teach you a lesson."

As Kaya followed Auntie back to the camp, she kept a strong hold on her feelings so that they wouldn't show, but her eyes stung with unshed tears. She kept her gaze on her feet when Auntie went to fetch Whipwoman, the respected elder selected to discipline children who misbehaved.

When Whipwoman arrived, she carried a bundle of switches. But it wasn't the switches that Kaya dreaded—it was the bad opinion of the other children. When one child misbehaved, all the children were disciplined. They learned that what one of them did affected all the rest.

"Come here, children!" Whipwoman called out. "Come here now!"

One by one, the children old enough to be switched came forward and lined up in front of Whipwoman. She laid her bundle of willow switches on the ground at her feet.

"Lie down on your stomachs and bare your legs," Whipwoman told them. She waited while everyone did as she said.

Kaya lay down, pulled her skirt up to her knees, and pressed her mouth to the back of her hand. She heard the switch hiss through the air and felt it sting her bare legs. She winced, but she didn't cry out or make a sound. Whipwoman moved on to Speaking Rain, then to the next child. On and on she went until they'd all been given a switching.

"A magpie that thinks only of itself would have given the boys better care than Kaya did," said Whipwoman.

As the children lay there, Whipwoman spoke to them slowly and firmly. "Kaya didn't watch out for her brothers. They ran off into the woods. They could have been injured. Enemies could have carried them away. A magpie that thinks only of itself would have given the boys better care than Kaya did! Nimíipuu always look out for one another. Our lives depend on it. Don't ever forget that, children. Now get up."

When Kaya lifted her head, she caught sight of her parents and grandparents looking on. Their sad faces hurt her much more than the stings on her legs.

Fox Tail got to his knees near Kaya. He grimaced as he rubbed his legs. "Magpie!" he whispered to her. "I'm going to call you Magpie."

"Magpie! Magpie!" echoed the girl next to him.

Speaking Rain inched closer to Kaya and clasped her hand. "Don't mind them," Speaking Rain said. "It's all over now."

But it wasn't over. Kaya thought with alarm, *Magpie! Is Magpie going to be my nickname? Will they never let me forget this?*

NICKNAMES

Chapter 4

"**THESE FISH NEED TO BE PREPARED,**"
Kaya's grandmother said to her. "Hold these sticks and
give them to me as I need them."

It was later that day, and Aalah was preparing a welcome meal for Kaya's family. She knelt on a tule mat with
several salmon in front of her. She was ready to cut up the
salmon and place wooden skewers in the pieces so that
they could be set by the fire to roast. Other women had
dug deep pits to bake camas bulbs in. The delicious scent
of roasting food filled the air.

Kaya was glad to be at her grandmother's side. Her
head still buzzed with all the trouble she'd caused. Kaya's
problems had started with her beloved horse.

"I raced Steps High, but she tried to buck me off," Kaya
confessed.

"Hmmm," Aalah muttered. She slid her knife up the
belly of a salmon, cut off its head, took out its innards, and
began to cut the rest into three long pieces. Her face shone
with sweat from the heat of the fires. Her hands glistened

with oil from the rich salmon.

One by one Kaya handed the skewers to Aalah. "But I'm going to train her," Kaya said, thinking out loud. "Someday I'm going to be the very best horsewoman!" When she heard herself boast again, she bit her lip.

"Hmmm," Aalah muttered again. She laced a skewer through a large piece of fish. "I've lived a long time, and I've known many fine horsewomen. First they cared for their families. Then they trained their horses. You must think of others before yourself." She held out her hand for another skewer.

Kaya bowed her head at her grandmother's lecture. She felt a tear run down her nose.

"What's wrong?" Aalah asked. She laid aside a piece of fish and reached for the next one.

"Some children are calling me Magpie. They say I'm no more trustworthy than a thieving bird," Kaya said miserably.

"Nicknames!" Aalah said. "Have I ever told you the awful nickname I got when I was your age?" Her hands never stopped moving as she spoke.

Kaya shook her head. She couldn't imagine her grand-mother doing anything to earn an awful nickname.

"Finger Cakes, that's what I was called," Aalah said. "Finger Cakes!"

Kaya couldn't help but smile. Women ground up kouse roots and shaped the mixture into little loaves, called finger cakes, to dry. Everyone liked dried kouse cakes. "That's a funny nickname," Kaya said. "Why did they call you that?"

Her grandmother picked up another large salmon. "My mother used to put a few finger cakes into my big brother's shoulder bag," she said. "If he got hungry when he was hunting, he'd chew on the finger cakes. I was jealous that he got extra pieces of my favorite food, so sometimes, when he wasn't looking, I'd steal some of his finger cakes. One day he caught me with my hand in his bag. From then on I was called Finger Cakes."

"Did they call you that for a long time?" Kaya asked.

"Yes, I was Finger Cakes for a long time," Aalah said. "Every time I heard that nickname, I remembered I'd been wrong to steal my brother's food. Every time I heard that nickname, I vowed I'd never again take what wasn't mine. It was a strict teacher, that nickname!"

"But you lost the nickname, didn't you?" Kaya said.

Her grandmother smiled. "Let me tell you something. Sometimes an old friend will call me Finger Cakes just to tease me. After all these years that name still pricks me like a thorn!" She put down her knife and wiped her hands on the grass. "These salmon are ready to roast now."

Kaya was still troubled. "Do you think I can lose my nickname, Aalah?" she asked.

Her grandmother looked closely at Kaya. Her dark eyes seemed to see right into Kaya's heart. "Listen to me," Aalah said. "You're not a little girl any longer. You're growing up. Soon you'll prepare to go on your vision quest to seek your *wyakin*. Work hard to learn your lessons so your nickname won't trouble you. Then your thoughts will be clear when the time comes for your vision quest." She pushed herself up from her knees. "These fish need to be carried to the fire. Everyone is hungry."

⊗◆⊗

Kaya's family gathered beside their tepee for their evening meal. Aalah had laid several tule mats in a row on the grass. The men took their places on one side of the mats. The women set wooden bowls of salmon and baked camas in the center and served the men. Then the women sat down across from them.

Kaya's grandfather led them in giving thanks to *Hun-ya-wat*, the Creator. *Kalutsa* held out his hands over the feast. "Are you paying attention, children?" he asked in a deep voice.

"Aa-heh!" Kaya said with the other children.

"Hun-ya-wat made this earth," Kalutsa said. "He made Nimíipuu and all people. He made all living things on the earth. He made the water and placed the fish in it. He made the sky and placed the birds in it. He created food for all His creations." After they all sang a blessing, each one took a sip of water, which sustains all life. Then they all took a tiny bite of salmon, grateful that the fish had given themselves to Nimíipuu for food. After that, Kalutsa motioned for the rest of the food to be passed.

As Kaya ate, she glanced from time to time at the others. She was surrounded by her grandparents, parents, aunts and uncles, and all the children in her family. She gazed at her father with his sharp cheekbones and broad shoulders. She looked at her mother with her shining black hair and her straight brows. Kaya felt how much she loved them all and how much she needed them. She wanted to be worthy of their trust, to be a girl no one would call Magpie ever again.

RIDING WITH TOE-TA

Chapter 5

"IT IS MORNING! WE ARE ALIVE!

The sun is witness to what we do today!" the camp crier called. He made his way among the tepees to waken everyone and announce the events of that day.

Kaya opened her eyes. Eetsa was already awake. She'd brought a horn bowl of fresh water from the river. Aalah was awake, too. She stood in the doorway of the tepee and faced the east, where the dawn sky glowed pink. With her eyes closed and her chin lifted, Aalah sang a prayer of thanksgiving to Hun-ya-wat, thanking Him for a good night's sleep and the new day. Kaya silently joined Aalah's prayer. Morning prayer songs were rising from all the tepees in the camp.

The prayers over, Kaya stretched and yawned. Beside her, Speaking Rain rolled onto her back and reached for her folded dress. The twins were sitting on the deerskin blanket they shared. They held out their hands for the root cakes Brown Deer offered them. Brown Deer had arisen before the camp crier passed by, too. Although Kaya hoped to be as hardworking and generous as her older sister, right now Kaya wanted to stay curled up under her soft deerskin as long as possible.

Aalah turned with a smile as if she guessed Kaya's thoughts. "Come girl, get up!" she said. "Roll up your bedding. It's time to bathe in the river."

Every single morning of the year, in cold weather as well as warm, all the children went to the river to bathe. The cold water made them strong and healthy. Grandmothers and Whipwoman watched the girls to make sure they got clean.

This morning Kaya delighted in wading into the quiet place at the river bend. A salmon tickled her toes as she walked out on the pebbly bottom to where the water reached her chest. As she splashed, the sun rose over Mount Syringa and flooded light into the green valley.

Rabbit, a girl older than Kaya, ducked underwater and came up next to her. She shook drops from her gleaming hair and gave Kaya a sly smile. "I didn't know magpies could swim," she whispered.

Kaya's cheeks burned. "I can swim, and faster than you!" she said.

"Will you peck me if you catch me?" Rabbit laughed. With strong strokes she began to swim for the shore.

Kaya swam after her. She could almost touch Rabbit's

flashing heels, but she couldn't catch up to her. Kaya waded out of the river with her head bent. "Magpie didn't win the race," Rabbit said with a grin.

That nickname stung like a hornet. *I let myself boast again!* Kaya realized with dismay as she dressed.

Kaya returned to their tepee, where she found her parents talking and laughing quietly together as Eetsa braided Toe-ta's thick black hair. When Eetsa had tied his braids together, Toe-ta beckoned to Kaya. "Let's go work with your horse," he said.

Toe-ta kept his best stallion, Runner, tethered on a long rope near the camp. He put a horsehair rope on Runner's lower jaw and mounted him bareback. He handed Kaya another rope bit and a long rope to carry. Then he lifted her up behind him on the big horse, and they set out toward the herd.

Kaya loved to ride with her father. She leaned against his warm back. The smooth gait of Toe-ta's stallion rocked them gently. "Toe-ta, Steps High tried to buck me off yesterday," she said.

"I thought so," Toe-ta said. "I saw you walking her. If you hadn't had trouble, you'd have been riding."

"I know your horse would never buck you," Kaya said.

Toe-ta was quiet for a little while. "Have I told you about the first time my father put me on a horse?" he said.

"You never told me that," Kaya said.

"Have I told you about the first time my father put me on a horse?" Toe-ta asked.

"I was a little boy, even younger than your brothers," Toe-ta said. "One day my father put me on the gentle old horse my grandmother rode. He told me to ride around the camp slowly. But after I went around slowly, I wanted to go faster. I kicked the horse as I had seen my grandmother do. The horse bolted! My father chased us, yelling to me to turn the horse uphill to slow him down. I looked for a soft spot and jumped off into the grass instead."

"Were you hurt, Toe-ta?" Kaya asked.

"I was sore all over!" he said. "Do you know why I told you that story today?"

"Why, Toe-ta?" Kaya asked.

"I want you to know that no one is born knowing how to ride," he said. "And you have to respect the horse you're riding. It takes a lot of work to learn what we need to know in this life."

Toe-ta swung Runner alongside a group of mares. Steps High was grazing with them.

"Whistle for your horse," he told Kaya. "She knows your whistle."

When Steps High heard Kaya's whistle, she pricked up her ears. As she came forward, Toe-ta tossed a rope around her neck and drew her close.

Each time Kaya saw Steps High, she marveled at her horse's beauty. Steps High was both graceful and strong, the muscles rippling under her skin.

Toe-ta got off his stallion and lifted Kaya down. As he approached Steps High, she tossed her small head and rolled her eyes. Toe-ta put the rope bit in her mouth and then grabbed a handful of mane as he swung onto her back. He held the rope reins firmly as he rode her away from the herd at a trot. Steps High pranced nervously, but she obeyed Toe-ta.

He drew the horse to a halt again by Kaya. "Now it's your turn," he said. "You're a strong rider. If you need me, I'm here to help."

Kaya swung up onto her horse. Toe-ta handed her the reins. But Kaya didn't urge Steps High forward.

"I won't push you too fast or too hard again," she whispered to her horse. "I want you to trust me."

Kaya pressed her knees to her horse's sides. She could feel a shiver run down her horse's back as Steps High began to walk. Steps High pushed against the bit as if she were thinking about running and bucking again, but she stayed at a walk until Kaya nudged her into a trot. Kaya kept her horse gathered in and rode slow circles until Toe-ta motioned for her to come to him.

He took her horse's reins in one hand and stroked Steps High's neck. "*Tawts,*" he said to Kaya. "That's just how you must ride her for a long time. Stay slow and stay in control.

Work with her a little longer and then come back to camp."
Toe-ta turned Runner and rode off.

As Kaya rode her horse in another circle, Fox Tail rode
up beside her. He'd been helping some older boys with the
horses. His face was dusty and his lips were dry. Herding
was hard work in the hot sun. "Do you want to race
again?" he asked Kaya.

"Toe-ta said I can't race my horse for a long time," Kaya said.

Fox Tail's grin was a wicked one. "I forgot that magpies
don't race!" he cried. He kicked his horse and galloped
away from her.

That nickname again! It gave Kaya a sick feeling in her
stomach. She clenched her teeth as she circled Steps High
back to the herd.

※◆※

The run of salmon up the river was
coming to an end. Many, many salmon
had given themselves to Nimíipuu.
The women had packed the dried
salmon into large woven baskets and
parfleches made of rawhide. Now they

parfleche

were packing up their belongings as well. Soon the women
would roll up the tule mat coverings of the tepees and take
down the tepee poles. They would put everything they
owned on their horses and the travois and set out. It was

time to move higher into the mountains so that the women could pick huckleberries and the men could hunt for elk and deer. Kaya and her family would be part of the group traveling back to Salmon River Country.

Aalah called Kaya to her. She looked worried. "I think I left my knife where we worked yesterday," Aalah said.

"I'll go look carefully," Kaya said.

Kaya already had a rope bit on Steps High. She'd been riding her horse every day, keeping her tightly reined in and held to a trot. Steps High hadn't once tried to buck off Kaya. But Kaya hadn't yet asked Toe-ta if it was safe to run her horse again.

"May I come with you, Kaya?" Speaking Rain asked. "I'd like to gather some of the elderberries along the riverbank." Kaya gave Speaking Rain her hand and pulled her sister up onto the horse to sit behind her. Riding bareback, they trotted away from the camp.

At the river, they passed Toe-ta and a few other men fishing for the last of the salmon. As the men speared fish, Fox Tail and some other boys put the salmon into baskets.

Toe-ta stood on the bank with his back to the sun. He had placed a large white stone in the current where the river was shallow. When a fish swam between the white stone and Toe-ta, he could see its outline and spear it.

Downstream, where the river was deeper, Aalah had

been cleaning fish on the bank the day before. Kaya reined in Steps High. "I'll start searching a little way down the path and make my way back to you," Kaya told Speaking Rain. "Wait here to mark where I started my search." Speaking Rain slipped off Steps High. As Kaya rode down the path, she looked for her grandmother's knife.

Steps High was tense and skittish. She shied at a garter snake crossing the path, but Kaya steadied her. When Steps High shied a second time, Kaya reined her in. "What's the matter, girl?" Kaya asked. "What's spooking you?" Steps High snorted and pawed the ground.

Kaya shaded her eyes and looked back to where Speaking Rain had been waiting. Speaking Rain was cautiously making her way through the elderberry bushes that grew along the riverbank. She couldn't know there was a steep bank on the other side of the bushes. "Stop, Speaking Rain!" Kaya called.

She turned Steps High and started back. Speaking Rain didn't seem to hear Kaya's call. Were Stick People leading her astray? She kept going. "Stop! Don't take another step!" Kaya cried.

Now Speaking Rain heard Kaya's cry. She stopped and turned. As she did, a piece of the bank crumbled beneath her feet. Speaking Rain fell backward. In a shower of stones, she tumbled into the swift river!

RIVER RESCUE

Chapter 6

KAYA DROVE STEPS HIGH FORWARD.
She jumped her over the bushes and reined her in sharply,
the horse's hooves plowing the ground. Speaking Rain was
struggling in deep water, trying to swim toward shore. As
she thrashed, a branch plunged down in the swift current
and hit her. She went under. When she came up again, she
was being pulled downstream in the powerful surge of the
river's current.

Fear struck through Kaya like a lightning flash. If
Speaking Rain wasn't pulled from the river, she'd drown.
If Kaya tried to swim after her, they could both drown. To
save Speaking Rain, Kaya's only hope was to run her horse
along the bank, try to get ahead of Speaking Rain, and ride
into the river to catch her.

Kaya gave her horse her head, then kicked her. Steps
High burst forward. In a few strides, she was at a full gallop. Kaya leaned low over her neck, clasping the horse with
her knees. What if another piece of riverbank gave way?
What if her horse bucked? Steps High lengthened out and

tore around the next bend, then the next. She seemed as swift as a hawk diving from the sky! Now they were ahead of Speaking Rain, who flailed in the churning river. From here, Kaya had to get her horse into the water and then swim upstream to meet Speaking Rain as she was swept down. Would Steps High obey Kaya's command to swim?

Kaya dug her heels into her horse's sides and again urged her forward. Steps High crossed the beach but paused at the edge of the water. "Come on, girl!" Kaya said, giving her another kick. Then Kaya felt Steps High become one with her again. The horse moved out into the icy current until she was swimming.

Kaya angled her horse upstream. She held tightly to Steps High's mane to keep her balance against the swirling currents. She'd have to catch Speaking Rain as soon as she came within reach, or else Speaking Rain would be swept under the horse's sharp hooves. In another moment, Speaking Rain was upon them. Kaya reached and grasped, caught her arm—she had her! She pulled and dragged Speaking Rain over her horse's withers. Holding Speaking Rain tightly, Kaya turned her horse downstream. She felt Steps High gather herself.

The horse's strokes evened out as she calmed. But Speaking Rain was limp against Kaya. Was she breathing? Kaya headed Steps High toward shore.

In a few more strokes, her horse's hooves touched bottom. Steps High's head came up, and she climbed onto the sandy beach. She shook her head and pranced a step or two as if she knew she'd done something to be proud of.

Kaya slid off her horse and caught Speaking Rain as her sister slipped down into her arms. Speaking Rain lifted her head, moaned, and began to cough up water. "You're safe, Speaking Rain!"

Toe-ta appeared on the bank above them. He was followed by the other fishermen and by Fox Tail. Toe-ta leaped down to the sand. He took Speaking Rain into his arms, bent her forward, and slapped her back with his cupped hand to force more water from her.

Kaya's teeth were chattering. "Speaking Rain, can you get your breath?" she asked.

"Aa-heh," Speaking Rain gasped.

"I heard you shout and I ran," Toe-ta said. "I saw what happened. You did well, Kaya. Your horse did well, too."

"Steps High knew Speaking Rain needed us," Kaya said. "She did everything I asked of her."

"She did what you asked because she trusts you," Toe-ta said. "You've earned her trust; remember that."

Fox Tail crouched on the bank. Was that a look of admiration in his eyes? "You told me you couldn't race," he said. "But you were racing like wildfire, Kaya."

"Kaya wasn't racing to be the fastest," Toe-ta corrected him. "She was racing to save Speaking Rain's life."

Toe-ta's words lifted Kaya's heart. He knew she hadn't acted for herself, but for Speaking Rain. And Fox Tail had called her Kaya, not Magpie!

Kaya closed her eyes, pressed her face against Steps High's warm, wet neck and felt the powerful pulse beating there. "*Katsee-yow-yow*, my horse!" she whispered gratefully. Then she held the bridle so that Toe-ta could lift Speaking Rain onto Steps High's back and they could take her back to camp.

※◆※

The horses needed fresh grass before they could begin the journey higher into the mountains. Kaya rode with Raven, Fox Tail, and some older boys and girls to herd the horses to new pasture. As Kaya rode, she gazed up at the tall peak. She knew the story of how the mountain came to be. An old chief had a vision. His vision told him that men with pale faces would come to steal the shining rocks scattered here. To protect their shining rocks, the people gathered them into a pile and built the mountain over them to hide them. Their treasure was saved because of the old chief's vision.

Kaya thought that if she'd lived in those days, she'd have helped build the mountain over the shining rocks.

After all, her name—*Kaya'aton'my'*—meant "she who arranges rocks." Her mother gave her that name because the first thing she saw after Kaya's birth was a woman arranging rocks to heat a sacred sweat lodge.

She knew that one day soon, like all the other boys and girls, she would go on her vision quest. *Will I be ready when that time comes?* she thought.

When she went into the mountains on her quest, Kaya would seek her wyakin. If her wyakin came to her, she could also receive special powers. Would the hawk give her the ability to see far? Would the canyon wren give her the power to defend her family, the way the wren drives off rattlesnakes? *What creature will my wyakin be?* Kaya wondered. She hoped it would give her powers and a vision to help Nimíipuu, like the old chief in the story.

Fox Tail rode past, his big roan kicking up a cloud of dust. *Fox Tail's too much of a rascal to become a leader of our people,* Kaya thought. But maybe the old chief, whose vision saved the shining mountain, had once been a bothersome boy like Fox Tail.

Will one of us be given a vision someday? Kaya wondered. *Will I?*

SALMON RIVER COUNTRY

Chapter 7

"LOOK, MAGPIE'S STEALING BERRIES!"

Little Fawn cried. "If she eats too many now, we won't have enough when winter comes!" She gave Kaya a teasing grin.

Kaya winced. Not a single day went by without someone calling her by her awful nickname—Magpie. Each time Kaya heard that nickname, it stung like Whipwoman's switch!

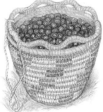

It was now late summer, and Kaya was back in Salmon River Country, where her family had joined her mother's band of Nimíipuu. They had traveled upstream and set up camp to pick berries in the higher country. Her father, her grandfather, *Pi-lah-ka*, and many other men had gone even farther into the mountains to scout the deer and elk trails. It was time for the hunt. Soon the men would bring back as much game as they could so that everyone would have plenty of meat for the winter. With the dried meat, fish, and berries, there would be good provisions for the cold season to come.

Kaya untied the basket from her belt and spread leaves over the berries to keep them from falling out of the basket. She set her basket with those her mother and her sister Brown Deer had filled. All the women and girls had been berry picking. Even the youngest girls wore little baskets— though they were allowed to eat many more berries than they saved.

Kaya's grandmother was loading baskets onto her horse. *Kautsa* glanced over her shoulder at Kaya and nodded at a little girl with her tiny basket. "Remember when you were that young?" she asked Kaya. "Remember how you'd run to give me the first few berries you picked?"

Kaya smiled, glad to be reminded of those happy days. "I remember you always praised me for my berries," she said. "You said I'd be a good picker one day."

"And you are!" Kautsa said. She hung the last bags onto her saddle and patted her horse. Leading it, she began to walk with the others down to the tepees set in the meadow near the stream.

Kaya walked alongside Kautsa, matching her strides to her grandmother's long ones. Heat rose from the stony path. "The sun's hot, isn't it?" she said.

"Aa-heh!" Kautsa agreed. "The day is hot and our work is hard. But we need to pick berries so we won't go hungry this winter."

Kaya studied the thick groves of lodgepole pines that ringed the meadow below. "Could Speaking Rain and I sleep outside the tepee tonight?" she asked. "I think we'd be cooler in the meadow."

"We'll be cool enough inside," Kautsa said. "I want you two near me. With many of our men away, we'll be safer if we stay close together. The boys are keeping the herd close by, too. Look, there's your horse along with the others."

Kaya shaded her eyes. She quickly identified Steps High by the star on her forehead. Kaya's horse was grazing at the edge of the herd with some mares and their foals. Perhaps Steps High sensed Kaya's approach, for she lifted her head and whinnied.

Kautsa halted her horse. She picked some large leaves from a thimbleberry plant beside the trail. Then she sprinkled a pinch of dried roots on the earth in thanks for what she'd taken. She used the leaves to wipe sweat from Kaya's forehead and then to dry her own face. "Go sit in the shade with Speaking Rain for a little while," she said. "The heat has tired you."

Kaya found Speaking Rain sitting under a pine tree. She'd stayed in the camp with the elderly women and men. She was weaving a beargrass basket that Kautsa had begun for her.

"I brought you some huckleberries, Little Sister," Kaya

said. She placed a handful of berries into Speaking Rain's outstretched hands. Kaya sat beside Speaking Rain in the shade of the pine tree. "Our dogs chased two black bears out of the berry bushes this morning," Kaya said.

"Everyone wants these berries," Speaking Rain said. She ate hers one by one, making them last as long as possible. As she munched, she tipped her head toward Kaya. "Why do you sound so sad?"

Kaya knew she couldn't hide anything from Speaking Rain. Maybe because Speaking Rain couldn't see, she heard everything sharply. "Little Fawn caught me sneaking huckleberries," Kaya admitted with a sigh. "She called me Magpie again."

"I hope that nickname will fade soon," Speaking Rain said. Again she cocked her head, listening. "Isn't that your horse whinnying to you? Go to her. Nicknames don't mean a thing to a horse!"

Gratefully, Kaya squeezed Speaking Rain's hand—Speaking Rain always understood her.

As Kaya walked toward the herd, she whistled her horse to her side. Steps High rubbed her head against Kaya's shoulder. Her horse's muzzle was as soft as the finest buckskin. "Hello, beautiful one!" Kaya whispered against the horse's sleek neck. It always comforted Kaya to stroke her horse.

As Steps High nuzzled her, Kaya glanced back at the clearing where women spread the berries on tule mats to dry in the sun. She saw her two little brothers bouncing on a crooked branch of a cedar tree, pretending to ride a horse. Nearby, little girls played with their buckskin dolls. Dogs lolled beside the tepees, their tongues out. In the wide meadow, boys rode herd on the horses. Thin clouds drifted toward the Bitterroot Mountains in the east. *Stay close to be safe*, Kautsa had reminded her. Kautsa was wise in these things, and Kaya had heard that warning all her life. But right now, this quiet valley seemed the safest place she could imagine.

A RAID IN THE NIGHT

⬧ Chapter 8 ⬧

"**LISTEN!**" KAUTSA SAID IN A LOW
voice. "The dogs are growling! Wake up!"

Kaya tried to waken in the deep of the night. She heard
Kautsa's sharp command, but sleep was like a hand pushing her down. Nearby, some dogs growled and then began
to bark fiercely. Kaya sat up and rubbed her eyes. What
was wrong?

Her mother peeked out the door of the dark tepee and
then ducked back inside. "Strangers in our camp!" Eetsa
said. "Get dressed! Quick! Enemies!"

Enemies! The warning was a jolt of lightning—swiftly
Kaya was on her feet. Her heart pounding, she struggled
into her dress. Kautsa, Brown Deer, and Speaking Rain
were doing the same. They all tugged on their moccasins
and crept out of the tepee. Kautsa pushed Speaking Rain
and the twin boys ahead of her. Brown Deer picked up one
of the little boys. Eetsa picked up the other one. "Follow
me!" Eetsa whispered. "Kaya, take Speaking Rain to the
woods! We'll hide there!" Crouching, Eetsa ran for the

trees, Brown Deer and Kautsa right on her heels.

The moon was rising above the trees bordering the clearing. Kaya could see women, children, and old people hurrying from the tepees for safety in the woods. Some men ran toward the edge of the camp, where dark figures ducked between the horses tethered there. Raiders! Enemy raiders! They'd slipped into camp hoping to make off with the best horses, but the dogs had given them away.

Kaya's mouth was dry with alarm. She clasped Speaking Rain's hand tightly. But instead of following Eetsa into the woods, as she'd been told, she went in the direction of the herd. Where was Steps High? Would raiders try to steal her horse?

Kaya saw the woman named Swan Circling head toward the horses, too. A raider was about to cut the rawhide line that tethered her fine horse. Swan Circling had as much courage as any warrior. She stabbed at the raider with her digging stick. She knocked him away from her horse, which reared and whinnied in panic.

The raider leaped onto the back of another horse he'd already cut loose. With a fierce cry, he swung the horse around and galloped straight through camp, coming right at Kaya and Speaking Rain!

With a gasp of fear, Kaya tried to run out of his way, pulling Speaking Rain behind her. Too late! Kaya threw herself onto her stomach, dragging Speaking Rain down with her. The raider jumped his horse over them and plunged on.

Kaya struggled to her knees. Now other raiders raced through the camp toward the herd. They lay low on their horses, trying to stampede the herd so no one could ride after them. The horses snorted and screamed with alarm. A few broke away. Was Steps High with them? Kaya whirled around. Nimíipuu men with bows and arrows were running to cut off the raiders.

Arrows hissed by. Kaya clasped Speaking Rain's hand again and ran for the safety of the woods. A horse brushed against her, almost knocking her down. She felt someone seize her hair, then grasp her arm. Speaking Rain's hand was yanked from hers. A raider swung Kaya roughly behind him onto his horse. She sank her teeth into his arm, but he broke her hold with a slap.

Kaya looked back for Speaking Rain. Another raider was dragging her onto his horse. "Speaking Rain!" Kaya cried, but her cry was lost in the tumult. The raiders raced after the herd, which ran full out now. The Nimíipuu men gave chase on foot, but they were quickly outdistanced.

Terrified, Kaya clung to the raider's back. The herd was thundering down the valley, the raiders in the rear. The night was filled with boiling dust. Hoofbeats shook the

*Arrows hissed by. Kaya clasped
Speaking Rain's hand and ran for the
safety of the woods.*

ground and echoed in Kaya's chest. She caught a glimpse of Steps High running with the others. Her horse had been stolen by the enemies. She was their captive, too, and so was Speaking Rain. And it was Kaya's fault!

All that night, and on through the next day and night, the raiders ran the stolen horses eastward. When their mounts tired, they paused only briefly before jumping onto fresh horses and continuing on. Kaya knew they wanted to get out of Nimíipuu country before they were caught.

Because the raiders didn't rest, Kaya and Speaking Rain couldn't rest either. The mountains and the valleys below went by in a blur. In her fatigue, Kaya sometimes thought she saw a blue lake in the sky. Sometimes she thought the distant, rolling hills were huge buffalo. And sometimes she did fall asleep, her head bumping the raider's back. He slapped her legs to waken her. She thought, then, about jumping off the running horse, but she knew she'd be injured or killed on the narrow, stony trail. *Maybe it would be better to die than to be a captive,* Kaya thought. But she couldn't abandon Speaking Rain.

When the sun was high overhead, the raiders finally stopped to rest. They left a scout to guard their trail and took the herd to a grassy spot by a little lake where the horses could feed and drink. Kaya saw Steps High standing by the water with the other foam-flecked horses. Their heads were down and their chests heaved from the punishing journey. How she wished she could go to her horse!

When the raiders gathered to share dried meat, Kaya got a better look at them. They were young, bold, and proud of themselves for stealing so many fine horses. She thought they spoke the language of enemies from Buffalo Country. Though Kaya couldn't understand their words, she knew that they boasted of their success. Perhaps they were proud, too, that they had driven the herd all the way through Nimíipuu country to the northern trail through the Bitterroot Mountains.

The raider who had seized Speaking Rain offered her some of the buffalo meat. When she didn't respond, he waved his hand in front of her eyes, then made a noise of disgust. Kaya knew he was angry that the girl he'd captured was blind. He pushed her down beside Kaya and stalked back to the circle of men. Kaya held her sister close.

Speaking Rain leaned against Kaya's shoulder. "Where are we?" she whispered.

"Somewhere on the trail to Buffalo Country," Kaya whispered back. She put some food she'd been given into Speaking Rain's hand.

"What will happen to us?" Speaking Rain's voice quavered.

Though Kaya trembled with fatigue, she kept her voice steady. "Don't you remember what happened when

enemies from the south stole some of our horses? Our
father and the other warriors got ready for a raid. As the
drummers beat the drums, all the women sang songs to
send off our warriors with courage. Our warriors followed
the enemies over the mountains and brought back all our
horses! Our warriors will make a raid on these men, too.
They'll take you and me back home with them. And they'll
take back all of our horses as well."

"Are you sure?" Speaking Rain murmured.

"Aa-heh!" Kaya whispered. "I'm sure."

But in her heart, Kaya was far from certain.

TAKEN CAPTIVE

※ Chapter 9 ※

KAYA SQUEEZED SPEAKING RAIN'S
hand. "We have to be strong."

"Aa-heh," Speaking Rain agreed. "We'll be strong."

Kaya and Speaking Rain lay side by side on the ground.
It had been days since the girls had been taken captive during an enemy raid on their village in Salmon River Country.

Their legs were tied together with a length of rawhide
so they couldn't run away. Huddled
together, they softly prayed to Hun-ya-
wat, the Creator, asking for strength.

The raiders had taken them
many miles from home. They were
now camped deep in the Bitterroot

Mountains after riding for days. Even though the girls
were exhausted, they were too afraid to sleep.

Speaking Rain put her cheek against Kaya's shoulder.
"Remember the lullaby that Kautsa used to sing to us?"

Kaya nodded. Then, to her surprise, Speaking Rain began to sing gently, "*Ha no nee, ha no nee*. She's my precious

one, my own dear little precious one."

Kaya glanced at the raiders—would they be angry at
Speaking Rain's song? The men were lying down to rest.
One glanced at Speaking Rain and shrugged as if he had
nothing to fear from a lullaby.

Lulled by Speaking Rain's gentle voice, Kaya slept.

※◆※

The raiders moved the herd eastward over the Buffalo
Trail as quickly as they could. As they rode, Kaya caught
glimpses of the Lochsa River in the valley, but the trail
stayed on the top of the ridge. The going was easier up here
than in the wooded gullies filled with windfall trees.

Kaya had been on this trail before. It was an old,
old pathway made long before Nimíipuu had horses. In
some places, it split and braided together again where
travelers had walked around fallen trees or boulders. In
other places, it was only a narrow ledge hugging a cliff.
Kaya watched the horses carefully when they came to the
dangerous ledges. Surely the raiders were pushing them
too fast along this treacherous part of the trail. A horse
that lost its footing would fall down the rocky slope and
perhaps be killed.

The gentle old pack horse that belonged to Kautsa often
stumbled in fatigue. Kaya kept her eye on the old horse,
hoping he could keep up. But on a curving ledge, the horse

slipped on some loose rocks. Kaya held back a cry as the old horse tumbled down the bluff in a shower of stones and lay still at the bottom. Wouldn't the raiders slow the other horses now? But no, they only pushed them faster. Kaya kept her gaze on Steps High and prayed that her horse would keep her footing. *Be strong!* she urged Steps High—and herself. Where were the enemies taking them?

Each night at last light, they camped in open glades where the horses could graze. A raider back-scouted the trail to see if they were followed. Kaya hoped that Toe-ta and other men were coming behind and would overpower the raiders. She thought that young men from Buffalo Country were no match for Nimíipuu men! But when the scout returned and the raiders continued on without rushing, Kaya knew no one was behind them.

At the highest point on the pass, Kaya gazed back at the mountains that loomed between her and her home country. She tried to find courage by remembering that Hun-ya-wat had made the sky above her and the earth beneath her. *I am in His home no matter where I go,* she thought. Still, fear was a bitter taste in her mouth as they moved farther from her people.

Each night the raiders tied Kaya's leg to Speaking Rain's. At first light, the raiders untied them and sent Kaya to gather heavy loads of wood for the fire. They fed Kaya and Speaking Rain only the scraps from their meals.

When they passed some hot springs, where steaming water spouted from the rocks, the trail ran down the east side of the mountains. The next day, they reached the broad river valley below. Kaya remembered passing this way with her family when they went to hunt buffalo on the plains beyond.

Then, this country had seemed full of promise and adventure. Now it seemed strange and menacing. A wide, swift river flowed north, down the valley. If the raiders crossed the river, they'd be well on their way to their home country. How would she and her sister get home from so far away?

In this valley, the raiders moved the horses at night to avoid being seen. Shortly after first light, they came to a small buffalo-hunting camp of their people, hidden in a canyon. The hide-covered tepees were decorated with animals and birds painted in brilliant colors—so different from the brown tule mat tepees of Kaya's people. As the raiders approached the camp, the hunters and the women gathered to greet them.

The raiders rode proudly through the camp, displaying

the horses—and the girls—they'd stolen. Though Kaya wouldn't let her feelings show, she was sick to see the raiders praised and honored. She winced when the men looked over the horses and stroked the ones they liked best, Steps High among them. How she hated to have enemy hands on her horse!

All the men and women in the camp were pleased and smiling, except one dirty boy with a sullen face who stared grimly at Kaya. She realized that the angry-looking boy was a slave, too, and that soon she and Speaking Rain would look as tired and bitter as he.

OTTER WOMAN

✷ Chapter 10 ✷

KAYA STARED AT HER FEET WHEN

the women came to inspect her and Speaking Rain. The
women pinched the girls' arms to feel their muscles. Then
they shook their heads and talked among themselves. They
didn't sound pleased.

Kaya and Speaking Rain were dirty and their hair was
tangled. They were used to bathing in the cold river and
cleansing themselves in the heat of the sweat lodge every
single day. Since they'd been captured, they hadn't been
able to wash.

When the women saw Speaking Rain's cloudy eyes,
they frowned and spoke angrily to the raiders. Were they
saying that a blind slave was nothing more than another
belly to feed? Would they decide that Speaking Rain was
no use to them and abandon her here, so far from Salmon
River Country? One raider took Speaking Rain's arm and
led her to a young mother with a baby. He said something
that caused the mother to look more kindly at Speaking
Rain. Kaya guessed he'd told the mother that the blind girl

wasn't entirely useless—she could sing lullabies and could help tend the baby while the mother worked. Kaya hoped they'd soon realize what a skilled cord maker and weaver Speaking Rain was, too.

One of the older women, with gray hair and a lined face, led Kaya to her tepee. Bold designs of otters were painted on the tepee in bright yellow and red. Kaya thought of the old woman as Otter Woman. She sat Kaya down and gave her buffalo meat to eat. When Kaya had eaten, the woman took Kaya to where other women were cleaning hides. She handed Kaya a sharp-edged rib bone and made a scraping motion. She wanted Kaya to scrape the fat and meat from a hide that was staked to the ground.

Kaya had often helped Kautsa clean hides. She knelt by the buffalo hide and began to scrape at it with the rib bone. Otter Woman watched her work for a little while, and then nodded in satisfaction. Kaya scraped even harder, until her shoulders ached and her arms were sore—she vowed to work twice as hard in order to make up for Speaking Rain. Somehow she must protect her sister.

When night came, Otter Woman led Kaya and Speaking Rain into her tepee. She spread hides for them beside her sleeping place and motioned for them to lie down. Taking a thick rawhide thong, she tied it around Kaya's ankle and then around her own. She made the knots tight so Kaya couldn't untie the thong and run away. She didn't bother to tie up Speaking Rain—a blind girl wouldn't try to escape.

Speaking Rain pressed against Kaya's side. "Be strong," Kaya whispered to her.

Otter Woman gave her a sharp pinch that meant, *Hush! Go to sleep!*

Kaya clenched her teeth and vowed she would not cry, not even in the dark. But how could she sleep when her heart was aching so badly? She and Speaking Rain were slaves—they might never see their people again.

At first light, Kaya was sent to gather firewood. She watched the hunters ride away from camp to hunt buffalo in the valley. Later in the day, when the men returned with the buffalo they had killed, they gave the meat and hides to the women. Otter Woman set Kaya to work and led Speaking Rain to sing to the baby.

All day the women worked, cutting up the meat and hanging the strips on poles to dry. They scraped and tanned the hides, wasting nothing. Kaya's arms and back ached from the hard work of scraping. When she grew dizzy from the sun and weary from the work, she told herself to be strong for Speaking Rain.

Black-and-white magpies swooped over the drying meat, stealing bits for themselves. Magpie—Kaya's

nickname. She had tried to be more responsible, but then she'd disobeyed Eetsa's order to run for safety in the woods.

That mistake had put her and Speaking Rain into captivity. *Maybe I deserve that nickname, after all,* Kaya thought miserably. She picked up a magpie feather and put it in the bag on her belt. It would be a reminder that she *must* think of others before herself.

From where Kaya worked, she often caught glimpses of Steps High grazing with the other horses. If only she could get to her horse, touch her, stroke her! Kaya watched for a chance to approach the herd, but the boys who tended the horses never left them.

One evening, when the sun blazed on the horizon, Kaya saw a horse move away from the herd and come nearer to camp. The horse was Steps High! The herders didn't seem to notice the lone horse, or maybe the sun blinded them when they looked her way. Kaya ran behind the tepees and into the sagebrush beyond the camp. She stopped there and whistled softly. Her horse raised her head and came over.

Before Kaya could reach her horse, a man strode up beside her, a rawhide rope in his hand. Angrily, he struck Kaya's legs with the rope and gestured for her to get back to the camp. As she turned to go, she saw him put the rope bridle on Steps High's lower jaw. Confidently, he leaped onto Steps High's back and rode away from the camp.

Kaya watched her beautiful horse galloping swiftly across the plain. *If only I could jump on your back and race away from here!* she thought.

TWO HAWKS

⚒ Chapter 11 ⚒

WHEN KAYA WAS SENT INTO THE
thickets to gather firewood, she sometimes brought
Speaking Rain along to help carry back the heavy bundles.
It was their only chance to talk freely.

"The hunt will soon be over," Kaya said one morning.
"They have almost as much dried meat as the pack horses
can carry."

"Aa-heh," Speaking Rain sighed. "It's getting colder,
too. Soon they'll start back to their country."

"If only we could escape before they take us farther
away," Kaya said.

"Aa-heh!" Speaking Rain agreed.

"But how can we?" Kaya asked. "We'd have to go when
it's dark, and at night I'm tied to Otter Woman."

"But I'm not tied up," Speaking Rain said. "Where does
she keep her knife?"

"In her pack." Kaya thought a moment as she wound
a thong around the armful of dry branches that Speaking
Rain held.

Speaking Rain was quiet, too. "Even if you cut yourself free, I'd never keep up with you on the run," she said slowly. "You'll have to go without me."

Kaya winced at the thought.

"You have to leave me." Speaking Rain's voice was firm. "You must escape so you can bring others back to get me."

Kaya pressed her fingertips to Speaking Rain's lips. "Don't say that! How could I go without you?"

"Because it's our only hope," Speaking Rain said.

※◆※

When Kaya and Speaking Rain came back to camp, Kaya saw the skinny slave boy tending a fire. There were burrs caught in his hair, and his only clothing was a ragged breechcloth and worn moccasins.

As she came near him, he motioned for her to stop. He glanced around, and then with his hands he threw her the words, *Do you speak sign language?*

Kaya had learned how people talked with gestures when they couldn't speak each other's language. She answered with her hands, *I speak sign language.*

What tribe are you? he signed.

She pointed to herself, then swept her hand from her ear down across her chin. *I am Nimíipuu,* her hands said.

I am Salish, he signed. Then he ducked his head because others came near.

Kaya went on to Otter Woman's tepee, but her thoughts were on the boy. Her people had many friends among the *Salish*. Some had even married Salish men and women. Perhaps she and the boy could find a way to help each other.

The next time she had a chance, she picked up some sticks and took them to where the boy was building a fire. Placing the sticks by his feet, she crouched beside him. She threw him the words, *What are you called?*

I am called Two Hawks, he signed.

She signed to him, *I am called Kaya.* "Kaya," she said out loud.

He narrowed his eyes and said slowly, "Kaya."

She nodded. Then she had an idea. Perhaps she and Two Hawks could escape together. Two would have a better chance to make it back to the Buffalo Trail and over the mountains than one traveling alone. Would he come with her?

And could Kaya trust this boy? She wished she could know him better before she risked telling him her plan— he might betray her to the enemies in the hope of being rewarded with more food.

Kaya waited for a chance. It came when she and Two Hawks were sent to bring cooking water from the river.

When Kaya was sure no one could see them in the

reeds by the river, she signed, *Pay attention to me! I'm going to go to Nimíipuu Country. Soon. Come with me to my family!*

His dark eyes bored into her. Then he threw her the words, *I want to go to Nimíipuu Country with you.*

Though his solemn expression gave away nothing, she realized he understood! *We will need hides. We will need food,* she signed.

He shook his head. *No! Let's go now!*

Kaya frowned. *This foolish boy!* she thought. If he acted recklessly, he'd put them both in danger. Didn't he know they'd have to wait for a dark night when they couldn't be seen? Didn't he realize they must plan ahead if they were to make it back safely? *Be patient!* She signed. *I'll give you a signal.*

Now! He repeated. Then he pointed to the horse herd not far downstream.

Kaya looked. Men were separating a few horses from the herd. Other men were tying bundles of buffalo hides onto the backs of horses. She saw that Steps High was one of the horses carrying a load of hides. *What are they doing with those horses?* she signed.

I understand their words a little, he signed. *They're going to trade those horses and hides to another hunting party. Then they'll leave for Buffalo Country. Soon! We must run away now!*

Kaya's mind was whirling—Steps High was going to be

traded away! Even now the men were riding off with the loaded horses. Steps High tossed her head and whinnied. She trailed behind the others as if she knew she was being taken far away from Kaya.

Grief was a knife in Kaya's chest as she watched her beloved horse disappear over the rise. Two Hawks was right—they must escape soon or be taken much, much farther from home country.

Kaya bit her lip. How could she bear to leave her sister and lose her horse as well?

ESCAPE!

※ Chapter 12 ※

Toward last light, the clouds turned red and the west wind blew more and more strongly. Kaya smelled the scent of rain in the wind. She heard small birds sing the high, whistling notes that meant a storm was on the way. By dark it would be raining hard, and everyone would stay inside the tepees with the door flaps closed. The storm would give her and Two Hawks a chance to escape.

When she saw lightning spike down from the clouds, she went to find him. He was banking the fires with ashes. She caught his eye and signaled to him, *Go! Tonight! Meet at the big tree!*

Soon rain lashed the tepees and thunder shook the earth. The dogs huddled down with their heads buried in their tails. Everyone except for a lone guard gathered inside. Otter Woman tied Kaya's leg to hers and settled down under several hides to sleep out the storm.

Kaya waited until she was certain everyone slept soundly. Then she whispered in Speaking Rain's ear, "The knife—in the pack beside the door."

Kaya felt Speaking Rain slowly inching away from their sleeping place. If she made any sounds, the wail of the storm covered them. After what seemed a long time, Kaya felt Speaking Rain's hand on hers, and then she felt the knife in her palm. Gently, Kaya began to work the knife against the rawhide thong—there, she'd cut it! She forced herself to lie still a while longer to be sure Otter Woman hadn't felt anything.

At last, Kaya eased herself away. To deceive Otter Woman if she woke, Speaking Rain took Kaya's place beside her.

Quickly, quietly, Kaya dressed, slid the knife into her bag, and folded up a sleeping hide. She put the little bag of food they'd saved into her bundle, too. Then her courage almost failed her—how could she leave her sister? She clasped Speaking Rain's hand. Speaking Rain squeezed back. Their touch was a vow that they'd be together again. Kaya dragged herself on her stomach under the edge of the tepee until she was outside in the howling storm.

The camp was shrouded in darkness, and the rain blew sideways. Kaya didn't see the guard—maybe he was checking the horses. She crept, keeping low to the ground, until she left the tepees behind. Then she began to run as she had never run before. She sped, wet sagebrush stinging her legs, until she made out the big cottonwood towering over the woods. Was Two Hawks there? Had he been able to escape, too?

As Kaya skidded down the slope toward the big tree, she slipped. She was on her hands and knees when she heard Two Hawks call softly from the bushes, "Kaya?" Never had her name been more welcome to her!

She didn't see the boy until he was right in front of her. In a flash of lightning, she saw that he carried a bundle and wore leggings he must have stolen from a raider. He beckoned for Kaya to follow and then started running across the open plain.

They ran westward into the wind. They had to cover as much ground as they could. As soon as it was light, the raiders would discover that their captives had run off. They'd follow swiftly on horseback. Kaya and Two Hawks must be well away and hidden by then.

All night they ran through lashing rain, but before first light the storm had passed over. Behind them the gray sky shimmered like an abalone shell. They ran along a rocky outcropping until they found a shallow opening beneath an overhang. Two Hawks dragged tumbleweeds over their tracks to cover their trail. Then they spread a hide under the rocky shelf, lay down on it, and covered themselves

*She didn't see the boy until he was
right in front of her.*

with the other hide. Two Hawks pulled a tumbleweed
into the opening to shield them. Kaya thought she was too
frightened to sleep, but in only a moment she fell into a
black slumber.

A hand pressed over her mouth woke her. Who held
her down? A raider? Then she realized it was Two Hawks
signaling her not to speak or move. She heard distant
hoofbeats. Then she heard the sound of horses running
not far from where they lay. Scouts had followed them!
Scarcely breathing, she pressed herself against the earth.
The hoofbeats became fainter and disappeared. Kaya and
Two Hawks had hidden themselves well. But would the
scouts find them on their return? The boy must have been
thinking the same thing. *Stay still!* He signaled to her.

All day they lay under the ledge. Slowly the light faded
and night returned. The enemy scouts hadn't come back.
Perhaps they'd given up their search, but there was no way
to know. Kaya and the boy would have to be on the lookout
every moment so they could see without being seen.

At last Two Hawks signaled to her, *Let's look around.*
They crept out of their hiding place like prairie dogs out
of a burrow. They ate some of their dried meat and sipped
rainwater from a hollow in a stone. Then they made their
way to the top of a low ridge and paused there to get their
bearings. The moon seemed to float up out of the dark lake

of waving prairie grasses. The stars were low and bright.

Kaya had been told many stories about the stars to help her find her way. She gazed up at the vast star map shining above them. She saw the group of stars called the Seven Duck Sisters. But she concentrated on the star that never moved, the North Star, called Elder Brother. With Elder Brother as a guide, she calculated the way west.

Follow me! she signaled to Two Hawks. He shook his head. Again she motioned for him to follow her, but he stayed put. *Does he think I can't read the stars?* Kaya thought. She stamped impatiently and started walking. Before she'd gone more than a few steps, he came after her.

All night they walked into the wind, which was rising and getting colder. They were near the foothills now, but they would never be able to discover the Buffalo Trail in the dark. They would have to chance moving by day if they were to find it. But first they must rest for a while. When the morning star appeared, Kaya signed to Two Hawks, *We need a lean-to for shelter.*

Enemy scouts might still be looking for them, so Kaya chose a spot hidden deep in a thicket. With the knife, she cut several branches from a pine and leaned them together to make a frame. Then she cut an armful of thick, short branches.

Help me, she signed to Two Hawks.

His lips turned down and his eyes were slits. *Building a shelter is the work of women,* he signed. *I won't do the work of women anymore!*

Don't you want to get warm? Kaya signed. *Come on, help me.*

You work, Two Hawks signed. *I'll keep a lookout.* He turned his back on her.

Kaya wove branches into the frame until the shelter was completed. She crawled inside, with Two Hawks right behind her. There was room enough for them to sit upright and eat the last few bites of their food. Kaya chewed slowly. Her belly ached with hunger and her legs shook with fatigue. As they wrapped up in their hides, her mind was filled with worries. Would they manage to find the trail again? Could they cross the mountains before snow blocked the pass? Despite her exhaustion, sleep was a long time coming.

DANGER

Chapter 13

Kaya woke to full sun and the
sound of geese. When she crawled out of the lean-to, the
last grasshoppers of the season sprang up around her.
Two Hawks stood grimly gazing up at the flock of geese
flying south. Did he know their flight meant snow could
be on the way?

Hunger made Kaya dizzy—surely Two Hawks was
hungry, too. She pointed to the dark mass of the foothills
ahead. She knew there would be fish in the streams that
ran through the hills. *Let's get some fish,* she signed. *Follow me!*

Two Hawks glowered at her. *Men lead and women follow.
You follow me!*

Kaya huffed in exasperation. But she decided not to
fight with him—maybe he wouldn't be so disagreeable
after they got something to eat.

Soon they were deep in the foothills. Kaya kept looking
back, but she saw no signs of enemy scouts. Perhaps they
were already on their way to their own country in the east.
Before her, the Bitterroot Mountains reached up to the sky.

Snow already covered the highest ridges. Kaya clutched her hide around her shoulders and shivered. She and Two Hawks didn't have much time. But she was so tired and hungry that her legs wobbled. She needed food and water, and she needed rest. *We must stop here,* she signed.

Two Hawks frowned. *We must go on!*

I can't go on, she signed.

He looked at her hard, his jaw set. *We have to go on!* he signed. He walked off as if he didn't care whether she followed or not.

If this skinny boy can keep going, then so can I! Kaya thought. She caught up with him, but they made slow progress. The woods were full of windfall trees they had to climb over. Twigs tore at Kaya's face and arms, and often she stumbled and fell. Then she heard the sound of a stream. Was this the stream that led to the Buffalo Trail? *We'll rest here and fish tomorrow,* she signed.

Two Hawks turned to her with a sullen expression. *Don't tell me what to do. My father is a warrior. Someday I will be a warrior, too.*

Right now you're only a boy! she signed. *And I know better than you.*

You're not the leader, he signed. *I am! I say we go on!*

Anger flared in Kaya's chest. It had been her idea to escape. If it hadn't been for her, he'd still be a captive. She was the one who had gotten them this far. She knew they'd never make it home if they didn't guard their strength carefully. *I say we build a shelter and rest!* she signed.

Two Hawks screwed up his face in a scowl. *I am not your slave! I am no one's slave anymore! I do as I choose!* He turned on his heel and started running alongside the stream. In a moment he'd broken through some bushes and disappeared.

Kaya was so upset that her heart was beating like a drum. How could this boy be so foolish! Should she let him go on alone or try to catch up with him again? She knew they'd be safer if they stayed together, whether he thought so or not—and she didn't want to face the night alone. So, against her will, she started plodding wearily upstream.

Kaya ducked under branches and climbed over rocks. When her head crashed into a cedar limb, she went to her knees in pain. *Let him go on if he wants,* she thought. *I need to rest.* Crawling on her hands and knees, she started to move under the cedar tree to sleep.

Her hand touched something warm and furry. What was it? She pushed back the branches and looked. It was the body of a fawn that an animal had killed. She knew that cougars hunted elk and deer in these woods. This was a fresh kill—the cougar that had made the kill must be nearby. Surely it would come back for its meal. But if the cougar came upon a running boy, it might think that he was more prey and go after him.

Kaya's first thought was to get away from the kill and hide—let Two Hawks look after himself! Then she thought of the Magpie feather in her bag. She'd kept that feather to remind herself that she must think of others first. She got to her feet and hurried upstream.

Around the bend she saw Two Hawks ahead of her on the pale, sandy shore. He was crouched at the edge of the stream, drinking from his cupped hands. When he heard her coming, he glanced her way. And as he did, she saw the flash of a cougar leaping down from an overhanging limb!

WORKING TOGETHER

Chapter 14

"LOOK OUT!" KAYA CRIED.

Two Hawks spun onto his side, and the cougar landed on the sand beside him. Kaya ran splashing up the stream, shouting and flapping her deer hide at the cougar. It clawed at Two Hawks's arms and shoulders. Kaya lunged forward and pounded her fist into the cougar's nose. With both hands, she grabbed handfuls of sand and threw them into the cat's eyes.

Blinking and snarling, the cougar released Two Hawks and began to back away. It was a thin, young cat with a lot of scars. Showing its teeth, it turned tail and retreated into the woods.

Two Hawks yanked off his deer hide. Kaya motioned for him to let her see the wounds on his arms. She washed away the blood and exposed the scratches, which were not deep. The deer hide he wore—and Kaya's quick action— had saved him from deeper slashes.

Kaya knew how to stop the bleeding. Although it was almost last light now, she found the plant called *wapalwaapal*, good medicine for his wounds. She silently offered a prayer of thanks as she made a poultice of leaves and packed it onto the cuts.

Then she sat back on her heels and drew a deep breath. *We must look out for each other,* she signed. *You and I are not enemies.*

No, we are not enemies, Two Hawks signed.

We have to stay together, she added. *We have to help each other.*

He nodded, his eyes downcast. *You did a good thing for me. How do you say "good" in your language?*

"Tawts!" she said at once.

After a moment, Two Hawks repeated, "Tawts. Tawts, Kaya."

When light came again, Kaya and Two Hawks made their way up the stream, looking for a good place to fish. Kaya's breath clouded at her lips. During the night, a skin of hard ice had formed along the shore. How much longer would snow hold off?

Here the stream widened into a basin before tumbling farther down. This was a good place to catch trout or mountain whitefish.

Kaya untied a piece of fringe from her skirt to use as a sniggle. She lay on her belly by the pool and dangled the fringe in the water. Fish would think the sniggle was food and bite into it. If she was quick, she could flip the fish onto the bank.

Two Hawks tugged a piece of fringe from the side of his leggings and lay down near her. He dangled the fringe in the water and waited. Almost at once, a fish bit the fringe. Expertly, he flipped a large trout onto the stones.

Soon Kaya felt a tug on her sniggle. With a flick of her wrist, she flipped another trout out of the stream and onto the bank. Good—they had enough for a meal.

I'll build a fire, Two Hawks signed.

Kaya watched him choose a sharp stick for a fire drill. He put the point of the drill into a hole in a dry branch. Then he rubbed the stick between his palms until tiny sparks fell onto dried moss. Soon a little flame burned, which he carefully fanned into a fire.

Kaya silently thanked the trout for giving themselves to her and the boy for food. Then she cleaned the fish and placed them on sticks by the fire to cook. When the fish were done, she and Two Hawks sat by the fire and ate them. She licked every bit of oil from her fingers. Never had anything tasted more delicious than this meal they'd made together.

As Two Hawks made a fire bundle to save the coals of their fire, a fine, cold rain began to fall. *Hurry!* Kaya signed. They had to find the Buffalo Trail before it was hidden by ice and snow.

As Kaya and Two Hawks made their way uphill, the

cold rain turned to sleet. Kaya pulled her deer hide over her head, but the sleet made it hard to see. She thought they'd been following the stream that would lead to the Buffalo Trail, but nothing here looked familiar.

After a time, the stream was nothing more than a small creek racing down the mountainside. Bighorn sheep leaped across ledges above them. Slipping on icy stones, Kaya and Two Hawks struggled upward. At last they reached the top. Two Hawks gave her a hand, and she climbed up on a trail that ran along the ridge.

The trail split around fallen trees—a path made by people on foot. Hoofprints were everywhere along it, too. *It's the Buffalo Trail!* she signed to Two Hawks. Her heart lifted—then she felt a stab of loss again. *If only Speaking Rain were with us!* she thought.

Up here the wind was bitterly cold. Kaya and Two Hawks put their heads down and started along the trail. Kaya saw horse droppings and the remains of fires, but the marks weren't fresh ones. With winter coming, travelers had already left the mountains for shelter in the warmer valleys. But Kaya knew enemies used this trail, too. *Keep a lookout!* she signed. How terrible if enemies should catch them now, with home country only a few sleeps away!

Wet and shivering, Kaya and Two Hawks worked to-gether to build a small lean-to against a rocky outcropping far off the trail. Because there was no water up here on the ridge, they scooped handfuls of sleet to suck.

If I had a bow and arrow, I could get us food, Two Hawks signed.

But there's hardly any game up this high, Kaya answered. We'd still have nothing to eat.

Then she saw that some pines were marked where people had stripped back the bark to get at the soft under-layer. The underlayer was food for both men and horses when they had nothing else to eat.

Here is food, Kaya signed. She began stripping back the bark with her knife.

As Kaya and the boy ate, wolves began to howl to each other across the ridges. Kaya and Two Hawks huddled together for warmth like puppies.

At first light, ice crystals glittered on frozen branches that rattled in the wind. Kaya and Two Hawks lined their moccasins with moss to keep their toes from freezing. Their fingers were blue and their teeth chattered when they took to the trail again, but during the night the sleet had stopped.

Even though she was cold, this old, worn trail com-forted Kaya. She felt the presence of the people who had passed this way before her.

After walking a long time, they came to a large cairn,

a pile of stones that marked a special place. People had built many cairns along the Buffalo Trail. The cairns marked sacred places where spirits were very strong. Two Hawks went on down the trail to scout their way, but Kaya stopped by the old cairn.

As she stood there, she thought she heard the voices of spirits. Were they reminding her that her name meant "she who arranges rocks?" Were they telling her to build another cairn at this sacred place?

She couldn't lift big stones, so she collected small ones and piled them up until she'd made a mound. She wanted to offer something of her own. She opened her bag and looked inside. There was the magpie feather she'd kept. "Magpie," her nickname. She tucked the feather under the top stone of the mound.

*She tucked the feather under the top
stone of the mound.*

FOLLOWING SIGNS

ALL DAY, AND ALL THE NEXT DAY, they climbed higher and higher. Kaya and Two Hawks looked around as they walked, often glancing up at birds and clouds for signs of the weather. Suddenly, Two Hawks pointed to a large tree far off the trail. There, high in the tree, was a platform of branches. A bundle was tied to the platform. Had hunters left food here for their return journey?

Two Hawks climbed up the tree to see. He came down with a rawhide bag slung over his shoulder. The rawhide was from the top part of a tepee, darkened from smoke that made it waterproof. *This is a Salish bundle,* he signed. *My people hunt on this side of the mountain. My people hid this food here!*

Eagerly they opened the bag. Inside were dried camas cakes and pemmican, a mixture of dried meat, fat, and dried berries. They sat under the tree to eat the tasty, nourishing pemmican. This unexpected find would give them strength to push on.

They were hurrying along the trail when Two Hawks signaled for Kaya to halt. *Look,* he signed. *Do you know that country?*

Kaya looked where he pointed. In the far, far distance, she could see what seemed to be a stretch of prairie. Was that the prairie where her people sometimes dug camas bulbs? If it was, they were closer to home country than she'd thought. *Soon we will be with my people!* she signed.

Come on! Two Hawks answered. *Let's get a better look.*

Kaya's heart was light as they scrambled up off the trail to a place where they could see more clearly. From up here, the prairie looked like a brown blanket laid over the land. Two Hawks was even more eager than she to see it. He climbed a tall pine until he was almost to the top, leaned out, and shaded his eyes.

With a sharp crack, the branch he stood on snapped under his weight! Crying out with surprise, he pitched backward and fell. He crashed down through the branches. With a thud, he hit the ground and tumbled down the hill on the far side. He cried out again, this time in pain.

Kaya rushed down to him. Clutching his ankle, he lay on his side. She crouched and saw a lump on his ankle. When she touched it, he gasped.

She handed him a stick to use as a cane. He seized the stick and tried to rise, but when he put weight on his

injured leg, he collapsed in pain. He tried again, only to
fall a second time. His face was wet with sweat from his
struggle. *My ankle is broken,* he signed.

Kaya bit her lip. She knew she wasn't strong enough to
carry Two Hawks more than a little way. Maybe he could
crawl a little way, too. But if he couldn't, how would they
get out of the mountains?

She hugged herself. What should they do now? The
cold wind whipped about them, and last light was coming
soon. They needed a shelter and a fire.

Kaya collected dry twigs and sticks and handed them
to Two Hawks along with the fire bundle he'd made.
Grimacing in pain, he unwrapped the coals in the fire
bundle and set about building a fire. As he worked, she
gathered branches and built a lean-to shelter. How she
wished for many, many hides to make the shelter wind-
tight! They had the Salish food, but Two Hawks was in too
much pain to eat. His teeth chattered and his whole body
shook. His eyes were wide with fright.

How could Kaya help him? She lay down against his
back and put her arms around him to keep him warm.
Still, he trembled violently, though he would not cry.

Then Kaya thought of the lullaby that Speaking Rain
had sung. Kaya put her lips close to the boy's ear. *"Ha no
nee,"* she sang very softly. *"Ha no nee."* When at last he did

sleep, he groaned over and over.

Somehow, Kaya slept, too. She opened her eyes to a white world. Snow was falling thickly. Glittering flakes filled the air and drove into the opening of the lean-to. Snow covered the ground and weighed down the branches of the trees.

Two Hawks tried to rise, only to collapse onto his side. Kaya knew she couldn't carry him on the steep and icy trail. She'd have to leave him, hurry on, and try to reach her people. If he stayed in the lean-to with some food, perhaps he wouldn't freeze before she returned with help.

She crawled out of the lean-to and looked up toward the ridge. Drifts of blowing snow were all she could see. By now, snow would have covered the Buffalo Trail as well.

As she stood in the whirling white, she saw a woman standing under a pine tree on the slope. The woman was tall and strong, like the woman named Swan Circling. She wore an elk hide over her shoulders, and snow glistened in her braids. Light surrounded her, like the sun shining on ice. While Kaya watched, the woman turned and strode up toward the ridge, looking back over her shoulder from time to time.

Kaya clutched her hide around herself and followed. Upward she climbed, wet snow falling on her shoulders from pine branches when she brushed against them. Snow fell onto her head and into her eyes. She wiped her eyes, and when she looked again, the woman was gone. In her place, a wolf stood gazing at Kaya with yellow eyes. She saw the black tips of its raised ears and its thick, yellow-gray coat. It watched her intently as she climbed up to the ridge.

When Kaya reached the top, the wolf trotted slowly down the slope on the other side. It paused now and then and looked back at her, as if waiting for her to come along. Was the wolf a wyakin? Kaya hurried after it, and then, with a bound, the wolf leaped down into the trees and disappeared.

"Wait for me!" Kaya whispered. With the wolf gone, the woods seemed much lonelier.

As she searched the hillside for the wolf, she saw something moving. She ducked out of sight behind a tree and peeked around through the veil of snow. Farther down the hillside, she made out a horse and a rider wrapped in a buffalo hide. Enemy? Friend? The rider led a pack horse and rode a large bay stallion. Could it be Runner, her father's horse? Could Toe-ta be here in the mountains?

Kaya went slipping and skidding down the hill, snow flying up around her feet. "Toe-ta!" she cried as she went.

"Kaya!" he called back, and turned the horses uphill to meet her.

Then he was leaning over, lifting her up, putting her onto his horse in front of him. He wrapped her in the warm buffalo robe he wore and held her close. "Daughter, you're alive!" he said. "And Speaking Rain? Is she alive, too?"

Kaya put her face against Toe-ta's chest. It was like a dream to be in his strong arms again.

"Speaking Rain's alive, but she's a slave of our enemies," she said. "I escaped with a Salish boy, but he broke his ankle. He's over that hill!" She pointed.

Toe-ta took fur-lined moccasins from his pack and put them on Kaya's cold feet. He pulled out another buffalo robe, wrapped it around Kaya's shoulders, and set her behind him on Runner. Leading the pack horse, they started back over the ridge to get Two Hawks.

Kaya clung tightly to Toe-ta's back. "How did you find me?" she asked.

"We searched and searched but found nothing," Toe-ta said in his deep voice. "Then two sleeps ago, a scout came to our hunting camp. He'd come down from the Buffalo Trail to the river because snow was coming. He told us he'd seen a new cairn at a sacred place along the trail. The cairn was made of small stones—ones someone with small hands might choose. Hands like yours, Daughter.

"The scout said a magpie feather was stuck into the

little cairn. I thought of your nickname—Magpie. I left our hunting camp and came up here to search for you. But if you hadn't seen me and come running, I wouldn't have found you in this snow. Were you watching the trail?"

"I didn't know where the trail was—" Kaya began, but then she stopped herself. She wouldn't speak of the spirit woman who led her away from the lean-to. She wouldn't speak of the wolf that had brought her in sight of the Buffalo Trail and Toe-ta either. If the wolf was a wyakin, she would not tell anyone until the proper time.

So much had happened to Kaya—how could she tell all of it? Where would she start? "Toe-ta, the raiders traded away my horse," she said.

"She's a good horse," he said slowly. "Perhaps you'll see her someday."

"And Two Hawks—can we help him get back to his people?" she asked.

"We'll help the boy join his people when the snow melts and it's time to dig roots again," Toe-ta assured her.

Kaya pressed her face to Toe-ta's back. She closed her eyes tightly and forced herself to say what she had to admit. "It's my fault Speaking Rain's a slave," she whispered. "I thought of my horse before I thought of Speaking Rain. But I made a vow I'd bring her back to us one day—somehow."

Toe-ta reached back and pulled the buffalo robe tighter around Kaya. "We'll do all we can to find Speaking Rain, but you must not blame yourself that you were taken captive," he said. "You were taken far from home, and you've endured much. But, Daughter, you are alive and well! Let us give thanks to Hun-ya-wat that you're with us again!"

GLOSSARY
✳ of Nez Perce Words ✳

PHONETIC/NEZ PERCE	PRONUNCIATION	MEANING
aa-heh/´éehe	AA-heh	yes, that's right
Aalah/Eelé	AA-lah	grandmother from father's side
Eetsa/Iice	EET-sah	mother
Hun-ya-wat/ Hanyaw´áat	hun-yah-WAHT	the Creator
Kalutsa/Qalacá	kah-luht-SAH	grandfather from father's side
katsee-yow-yow/ qe´ci´yew´yew´	KAHT-see-yow-yow	thank you
Kautsa/Qáaca´c	KOUT-sah	grandmother from mother's side
Kaya´aton´my´	ky-YAAH-a-ton-my	she who arranges rocks
Nimíipuu	nee-MEE-poo	The People; known today as the Nez Perce

In the story, Nez Perce words are spelled so that English readers can pronounce them. Here, you can also see how the words are spelled and spoken by the Nez Perce people.

PHONETIC/NEZ PERCE	PRONUNCIATION	MEANING
Pi-lah-ka/Piláqá	pee-LAH-kah	grandfather from mother's side
Salish/Sélix	SAY-leesh	friends of the Nez Perce who live near them
tawts/ta´c	TAWTS	good
tawts may-we/ ta´c méeywi	TAWTS MAY-wee	good morning
Toe-ta/Toot´a	TOH-tah	father
Wallowa/ Wal´áwa	wah-LAU-wa	Wallowa Valley in present-day Oregon
wapalwaapal	WAH-pul-WAAH-pul	western yarrow, a plant that helps stop bleeding
wyakin/wéeyekin	WHY-ah-kin	guardian spirit

*Bear Blanket studied the baby's face and
bent over to listen to her coughing.*

❆ A Sneak Peek at ❆
SMOKE
ON THE WIND

"**Y**OUR BABY NEEDS MEDICINE NOW,"

Swan Circling said. Bear Blanket wants me to bring her the inner bark of a special tree to boil for a healing drink," she said to Running Alone, the baby's mother.

Running Alone put her hand on Swan Circling's arm. "Then hurry!" she urged her. "Kaya will round up your horse for you while you get your blankets and your knife."

Kaya threw a deerskin over her shoulders and grabbed a rope bridle. Her breath was a white plume at her lips as she ran out to the herd grazing near the village. She found Swan Circling's white-faced horse, placed the bridle on her lower jaw, and rode her back to the lodges.

Swan Circling was wearing otter-skin leggings and mittens and had her elk robe around her. She held her beautiful saddle of wood and painted rawhide. Kaya reined in the horse and slipped off. She put on the saddle and reached under the horse's belly for the cinch. Already Swan Circling was hanging her bags from the saddle horn.

"Cinch it snugly," Swan Circling told Kaya. "I'm going to ride as fast as possible. Bear Blanket said the baby is very sick." She tested the saddle cinch with her weight and then swung up. "Good work, Kaya. I'll be back before last light. Watch for me." She urged her horse forward and, in a few strides, was running full out across the frozen ground.

"I'll watch for you!" Kaya called after her. But the wind snatched away her words.

All day Kaya stayed with Running Alone and her baby. Bear Blanket sang her medicine songs, but the baby only coughed harder and harder. Her little face was red, and her eyes screwed shut with her effort to breathe. Kaya watched her anxiously—did the baby have the terrible sickness of blisters that the men with pale faces had brought to the land? Kaya was afraid to ask.

As the light began to fade, Kaya went to watch for Swan Circling's return. At dusk there were no colors in the valley. The river was a shining black curve, like a snake, and the trees were black slashes against the white snow. Under dark clouds, a hawk rode the wind in slow, wide turns. *Where is Swan Circling?* Kaya thought. *Why doesn't she come back?*

Then she saw a horse appear in the trees at the far end of the valley. Kaya ran up the hillside a little way to get a better look. The horse had a white face—Swan Circling's horse. Kaya caught her breath in relief. But as the horse came closer, out of the trees, Kaya saw that it was limping as though it was hurt—and that it had no rider.

FOR COUNTLESS GENERATIONS,

grandparents have told children like Kaya stories for fun and for education. Through stories about a character named Coyote as well as other animals, Nimíipuu children learned about the world around them, how to behave and how not to behave, and the tradtions of their people. Elders told children this story to explain how Nimíipuu believe they—and other people—came to be:

Coyote is an important character in hundreds of legends.

According to legend, long before there were any humans on the earth, the animals could talk, and they acted like people. One day, a greedy monster came along and started eating everything in its path. After a while, Coyote decided the time had come to stop the monster. He hid a bone knife in his mouth and tricked the monster into swallowing him. Once Coyote was inside the monster, he used his knife to cut out the monster's heart. The

monster died, and all the animals he had swallowed escaped.

Near Kamiah, Idaho, you can visit the Heart of the Monster landmark.

Coyote cut the monster into pieces and flung them to the four winds. Wherever a piece landed, a group of humans was born. After all the pieces of the monster had been scattered, Fox pointed out that Coyote had not put any humans in the beautiful spot where he and Coyote were standing. So Coyote sprinkled some blood from the monster's heart on the ground. From the monster's lifeblood sprang the last group of humans—Nimíipuu, which means "The People."

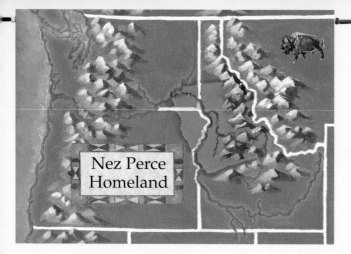

Nez Perce
Homeland

In the 1750s, the Nez Perces' territory, shown on the map in red, covers about 27,000 square miles of modern-day Idaho, Washington, and Oregon

Today, Nimíipuu are known as the Nez Perce, which is French for "pierced nose." Early white explorers, including French fur trappers, mistakenly believed that all Nez Perce wore shells through their noses and gave them that name.

As a girl, Kaya's classroom was the world around her, and family members were her teachers. She and her band traveled with the seasons to gather food and to hunt and fish. While traveling, Nez Perces set up temporary camps of small tepees. Then, every fall, the people settled back into their permanent villages in the warmer valleys along rivers and streams.

Kaya started each day with a prayer to Hun-ya-wat, the Creator, for all the living things around her as well as the earth, the sky, and

Girls laced their dolls into toy cradleboards the same way mothers laced babies into real cradleboards.

These girls from the early 1900s are building play tepees just as Kaya did. In Kaya's time, play tepees were important practice—women were responsible for building their families' homes.

the water. Nez Perces believed that everything Hun-ya-wat created had spirits and special powers. Guardian spirits, called wyakins, gave these special powers to humans through visions and helped them throughout their lives. Kaya's people believed that their spirits were part of the land—a land of rugged peaks and deep canyons, dense forests and vast grasslands, gently rolling hills and swift-moving rivers. For thousands of years, Kaya's people had taken care of the land, and it had given them everything they needed to survive and grow strong.

Young girls helped make decorative horse trappings. Dangling shells jingled in time with the horse's trot. Small feathers or beads embellished bridles. Each horse was dressed as uniquely as the girl who rode it.

By the time Kaya turned nine years old, she would learn how to cook food and prepare it for winter storage. She would learn how to soften the hides of animals and make clothes and moccasins from the prepared skins. She would learn how to weave baskets and paint bags called *parfleches*, and she would begin to learn how to help build and furnish a home for her own family one day.

Nez Perce children learned to recognize—and avoid—the markings of dangerous animals such as rattlesnakes and grizzly bears. They learned that swallows signaled the return of the spring salmon and the frogs' song meant that warm weather was on the way. They learned to identify landmarks that showed the way to the best root-digging fields and fishing spots.

Children were taught to be clean and trained to be strong. Every morning—in all seasons—they bathed in a stream, and every evening they cleansed themselves in a sweat lodge. They were active constantly, running foot races, riding horses, and playing ball games.

Riding and handling horses was a particularly important skill to Nez Perces, who learned to be comfortable in the saddle as young as age three. They bred horses for speed, endurance, strength, and sure-footedness. Many of the horses had the striking spotted coats of the horses now known as *Appaloosas*. Horses allowed Nez Perces to travel farther and faster and to carry more goods. Horses were a sign of wealth, but they were also well loved, just as Kaya loved Steps High. The Nez Perce treated their horses with great respect. Still today, they honor their horses with decorated collars and saddlebags and parade their horses to show pride in Nez Perce history and culture.

A modern Nez Perce girl and her horse wear regalia, or outfits, that show pride in Nez Perce artistry.